FOCUS ON EUROPE

BELGIUM, LUXEMBOURG, AND THE NETHERLANDS

ED NEEDHAM

STARGAZER BOOKS

© Aladdin Books Ltd 2005

New edition published in the United States in 2005 by:
Stargazer Books
c/o The Creative Company
123 South Broad Street
P.O. Box 227
Mankato, Minnesota 56002

Printed in U.A.E.

Designer	Flick, Book Design and Graphics
Series Director	Bibby Whittaker
Editors	Jim Pipe
	Mark Jackson
Picture Research	Brooks Krikler Research
Illustrator	Dave Burroughs

The author, Ed Needham, has traveled extensively in Europe and has published several books on European countries.

The consultant, Henk Bakker, was born in the Netherlands and has a degree in philosophy. He now lives and works in Britain.

Library of Congress Cataloging-in-Publication Data

Needham, Ed.
  Belgium, Luxembourg, and the Netherlands / by Ed Needham.
    p. cm. -- (Focus on Europe)
  Includes index.
  ISBN 1-932799-13-3 (alk. paper)
    1. Benelux countries--Juvenile literature.
  I. Title. II. Series.

DH18.N44 2004
949.2--dc22

2004040808

INTRODUCTION

Belgium, the Netherlands, and Luxembourg —the Benelux countries—lie at the heart of northern Europe. Despite a history of repeated invasion by foreign powers, they have each retained a unique culture, and together they maintain a global importance far in excess of their size. The landscape, from the flat Dutch polders to the wooded mountains of the Ardennes, is as varied as the people who inhabit it. This book offers an insight into the Benelux countries and peoples, combining information from the fields of geography, language and literature, science and math, history, and the arts. The key below shows how the subjects are divided up.

Geography
The symbol of the planet Earth shows where geographical facts and activities are to be found. These sections include a look at the beautiful Ardennes region and the techniques used to reclaim land from the sea.

Spiere
Spiere - Helkijn
Espierres
Espierres - Helchin

Language and literature
An open book is the sign for activities that involve language and literature. One such panel looks at Dutch words that have come into common use in English, while another explores the language frontier in Belgium. A further panel highlights the two famous Belgian authors Hergé and Georges Simenon.

Science and math

The microscope symbol indicates where a science project or science information is given. If the symbol is tinted green, it signals an environmental issue. One panel looks at the Dutch approach to the environment.

History

The sign of the scroll and hourglass shows where historical information is given. These sections look at key events in the history of the Benelux countries and their impact on society.

Social history

The symbol of the family indicates where information about social history is given. Descriptions of rural and city life create a flavor of Benelux today.

Arts, crafts, and music

The symbol showing a sheet of music and artist's tools signals arts, crafts, or musical activities. Topics covered in this category include the Luxembourg-born botanical artist Redouté, the inventor of the saxophone, and a project to build a model windmill.

CONTENTS

THE BENELUX COUNTRIES

Belgium, the Netherlands, and Luxembourg are small, densely populated nations in northwestern Europe, collectively known as the Benelux countries (the Benelux flag is on the left). For centuries, these countries were ruled by the same foreign powers but, since gaining independence, they have played an important role in Europe and as colonial powers in countries such as the Congo and Indonesia. Over the last fifty years, they have grouped together economically to exploit their position at "the crossroads of Europe."

THE NETHERLANDS

BELGIUM

LUXEMBOURG

Luxembourg
The Grand Duchy of Luxembourg covers just 998 square miles and has a population of around 450,000. Osling, the northern region, is wooded and hilly, while Gutland, in the south, is flatter. As a tax haven, Luxembourg (below) is also a major center for commerce and banking.

The Netherlands
The Kingdom of the Netherlands is often mistakenly called Holland, which in fact is only a region within the country. The Kingdom occupies 13,104 square miles, and has a population of over 16 million. The word Netherlands means "low countries"—it is mostly flat, with much of the land below sea level.

Belgium
The Kingdom of Belgium covers 11,787 square miles and has a population of over 10 million. It is often described as being the shape of a bunch of grapes. Like the Netherlands, much of Belgium is low-lying and linked by a complex system of canals. The Ardennes region, in the southeast, is more mountainous. The capital, Brussels (the Grand Place is shown left), is both a major commercial and industrial center and home to the European Parliament.

Population pressure

The Benelux countries are among the most densely populated areas in the world. The Netherlands averages 745 people per square mile, compared to 386 per square mile in the U.K. and just 43 per square mile in North America. This tends to mean busy streets, crowded highways, and very few large areas of open land without any buildings. In all three countries, the vast majority of the population is urban.

Place in Europe

The Benelux countries form a wedge in north-western Europe with the North Sea to the west, north Germany to the east, and France to the south-west. Britain is a short journey across the North Sea. They have long exploited their position by building their prosperity on trade with these three large neighbors.

Language frontiers

The Benelux countries are a patchwork of language groups. In the Netherlands, people speak Dutch, except in Friesland, where they speak Frisian. Luxembourg has its own language, Letzeburgesch, though French and German are official languages, too. Belgium is split into Flanders, where they speak Flemish (a form of Dutch), and Wallonia, where they speak French. A minority speak German.

Why are they important today?

After the Second World War, Belgium, the Netherlands, and Luxembourg formed the Benelux Customs Union. This made trade easier between them, and helped them operate as a stronger block in competition with larger nations. They made up three of the six countries to sign the Treaty of Rome in 1957, which brought the Common Market into being. This has since developed into the European Union.

NETHERLANDS

Flanders

Brussels

Wallonia

BELGIUM

Fr/Flemish

German

Dutch

French

LUXEMBOURG

EARLY HISTORY

The flat countryside has made the region easy for foreign powers to invade. The Romans arrived in 58 BC, led by Julius Caesar, conquering all the land up to the Rhine. During the 14th century, the French house of Burgundy and then the Austrian house of Hapsburg took control, both attracted by the area's prosperity. In the 16th century, Protestantism reached the northern provinces (the modern Netherlands), which split away, while Belgium and Luxembourg remained under the Catholic Spaniards.

Date chart

4000 BC	Region settled by Celts. (A Celtic bracelet is shown at the top of the page.)
58 BC-400 AD	Belgium and some of the Netherlands under Roman rule.
481-843	Franks control the region.
768	Pope declares the Frankish king Charlemagne (left) Emperor of the West.
10th century	Independent duchies, counties, and towns established. Cloth trade makes the area prosperous. Start of the use of waterways.
14th-15th centuries	French dukes of Burgundy take control and unite the area.
1477	Through a marriage alliance, the Low Countries (a term referring to what are now the Benelux countries) pass to the Austrian Hapsburg family.
1516	The Low Countries become a Spanish possession, under Charles V.
1566	Revolt of the Netherlands begins. Protestants become fed up with harsh Spanish rule of Philip II. Revolt led by William the Silent, Prince of Orange.
1581	The Dutch declare their independence from Spain. Belgium and Luxembourg remain Catholic and under Spanish control.
17th century	The Netherlands becomes world's leading sea power.
1648	Spain finally recognizes Dutch independence.

A Peasant Wedding—instead of the biblical scenes favored by his contemporaries, Pieter Brueghel the Elder (1520-69) painted pictures of ordinary people, showing how they lived and how towns and villages looked in the 16th century.

Cloth guilds

In the Middle Ages, the clothworking trade made cities like Ghent and Bruges among the richest in Europe. Feudal lords gave charters to merchant guilds. These gave the merchants special privileges and made them rich and powerful. To join a guild, it was necessary to serve an apprenticeship of several years, and no one could trade without belonging to the guild.

Belgae tribe
"Of all the people of Gaul," said Julius Caesar, "the Belgae are the bravest." The Romans defeated this Celtic tribe in 57 BC, and called the area Belgica. In the 3rd century AD, Belgium was divided between Germans in the north and Celts in the south—the origin of its language split.

Burgundians and Hapsburgs
Prior to the 11th century, foreign rulers took little interest in the Low Countries. But when thriving fishing, shipping, and textile industries developed, the French dukes of Burgundy were quick to take control. They achieved this by a combination of inheritance, marriage, money, and war. Under the Burgundians, trade and the arts continued to flourish in the region. Through marriage, authority passed to the Austrian Hapsburgs in 1477, but in 1506, the region came under Charles V, King of Spain, who was born in Ghent. People said his empire was so vast that the sun never set on it. When the Netherlands split off, Belgium and Luxembourg remained Hapsburg dominions until Napoleon invaded in 1795.

MARIE DE BOURGOGNE, *fille de Charle le Hardi.*

When Mary of Burgundy (left) married Maximilian I in 1477, the Low Countries came under Hapsburg control.

William the Silent
William, Prince of Orange, was a moderate man who was horrified by the brutal Spanish regime of Philip II. He led the Revolt of the Netherlands, which began in 1566.

Reformation era
The Reformation was a 16th-century movement to reform the Church. Many felt that the Catholic Church had grown corrupt, and preferred the austere Protestant beliefs of Martin Luther and John Calvin. The Spanish considered themselves defenders of the Catholic faith, and were incensed by the spread of Protestantism. Charles V's son, King Philip II (right), tortured, imprisoned, and executed Protestants to try and control them. But the Dutch grew rich, despite long wars against the Spanish, and they achieved full independence in 1648.

7

INDEPENDENCE ONWARD

The Dutch Golden Age came to an end in 1714, a year after Belgium and Luxembourg passed from Spanish back to Austrian control. At the end of the century, all three countries were conquered by Napoléon (left), and after his fall they were grouped together as the Kingdom of the Netherlands, until Belgium and Luxembourg won their independence in 1830. After the destruction of two world wars, the three countries formed the Benelux Customs Union in 1947, to give them a better trading position.

Waterloo
Waterloo, a town near Brussels, saw Napoléon's final defeat in 1815. After returning from exile on Elba, he fought on for a hundred days, until defeated by an army under Wellington.

Leopold I
Leopold I became the first King of the Belgians in 1831. Despite constant friction between Walloons and Flemings, Leopold's diplomacy held together the fledgling country, which powerful neighbors threatened to devour.

A colonial past
The Netherlands colonized Indonesia and Surinam in the 17th century. Indonesia was the base for the Dutch East India Company's trade with the Orient. The Dutch captured the Caribbean islands of Aruba and Antilles from the Spanish in 1634, plus land around New York (then called New Amsterdam). Dutch settlers also founded the Cape colony in 1652—the Afrikaaners are their descendants. In the 19th century, Belgium colonized the African countries of Congo, Rwanda, and Burundi.

A bridge too far
One of the most daring actions of the Second World War took place in the Netherlands, when 35,000 troops were dropped near the town of Arnhem in an attempt to capture the bridge over the Rhine. But the plan failed due to poor intelligence and many paratroopers died needlessly.

Wartime heroines

Anne Frank (1929-45) was a German Jew whose family fled to Amsterdam to escape the Nazis in 1933. During Nazi occupation of the Netherlands, they hid in a secret room until they were betrayed. Anne died in Belsen concentration camp. Her diary was published in 1947 and made into a film. Queen Wilhelmina of the Netherlands (1880-1962) won the admiration of her people during the war because of her constant encouragement of the Dutch resistance.

The site of the First World War battlefield of Ypres (above)

Modern-day Luxembourgers celebrate the gaining of independence in 1830.

Date chart

1652-74	The Netherlands fight three naval wars with England to keep control of the seas.
1701-14	The Dutch lose control of the seas to England, following war with France.
1713	Following the War of the Spanish Succession, Luxembourg and Belgium return to the Austrian Hapsburgs.
1795	Napoléon invades. The Netherlands becomes the Batavian Republic, and Belgium and Luxembourg are annexed to France.
1815	The Congress of Vienna joins the three countries in the Kingdom of the Netherlands.
1830	Belgium and Luxembourg declare their independence.
1914-18	Belgium fights against Germany in the First World War. The Netherlands remains neutral.
1940-45	Germany occupies the Benelux countries during the Second World War.
1957	The three countries help establish the European Common Market.
1971	Belgian constitution divides country into three communities based on language.
1980	Belgian Parliament grants partial autonomy to Flanders and Wallonia.
1992	Belgium, Luxembourg, and the Netherlands sign the Maastricht Treaty.
2002	Belgium, Luxembourg, and the Netherlands join the European single currency.

The Atomium

The Atomium stands in the Exhibition Park in Brussels, and has become a symbol of the city. It is an aluminum model of a carbon molecule magnified 165 billion times, and it was built for the 1958 World's Fair. It was designed by the Belgian architect Eugene Waterkeyn. The spheres are connected by escalators.

At its highest point, the Atomium (right) is 394ft above ground.

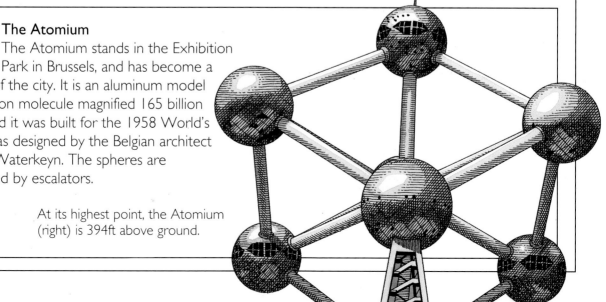

BELGIAN CITIES

As many as 97 percent of Belgians live in towns or cities. Brussels is the largest Belgian city and, together with its suburbs, is the only one with a population of over a million. Brussels is bilingual and claims to be the capital of Europe, with the European Parliament and hundreds of international companies and organizations located there. Belgian towns (a typical town square is shown above left) are linked by the world's densest railroad network, and by highways that emanate from Brussels like spokes, which are easily identifiable from the air.

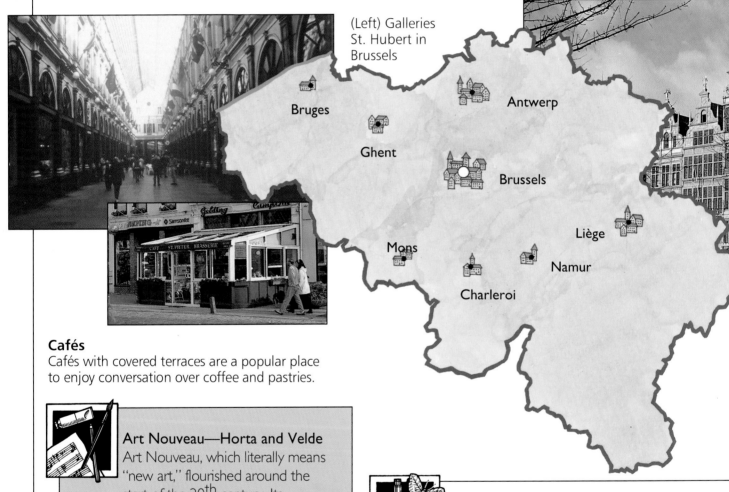

(Left) Galleries St. Hubert in Brussels

Bruges

Ghent

Antwerp

Brussels

Liège

Mons

Namur

Charleroi

Cafés
Cafés with covered terraces are a popular place to enjoy conversation over coffee and pastries.

Art Nouveau—Horta and Velde
Art Nouveau, which literally means "new art," flourished around the start of the 20th century. Its characteristic plant and flower patterns and elegant curling lines became fashionable in architecture and the decorative arts. Baron Victor Horta (1861-1947), a Belgian architect, was one of the originators of Art Nouveau, as was Henri Clemens van de Velde (1863-1957), who designed furniture, ceramics, metalwork (right), and textiles.

Belgian chocolates
Belgian chocolates by manufacturers such as Godiva, Neuhaus, and Gartner are famous the world over for their quality. One reason why Belgian chocolates taste so good is because of the high percentage of milk fats used. One of the qualities of milk fats is that they melt just below body temperature, making them melt as soon as you put them in your mouth!

Antwerp

Antwerp, the largest city in Flanders, was once the hub of an international trading empire. With the decline of Bruges in the late 15th century, Europe's great trading families moved to Antwerp. Its Golden Age lasted less than 100 years, and the city declined until Napoléon revived its docks as "a pistol pointed at the heart of England." Today, it is the center of the world's diamond trade.

The Money Lender and his Wife (above). This painting by Massys (c.1466-1530) illustrates Belgium's long association with gold and precious stones—Bruges was Europe's first money exchange.

Antwerp's central square (left)

Belgian constitution

Belgium is a parliamentary democracy, governed by rules first established by the 1830 constitution. The king is the head of state. Since 1970, some powers have been given up by central government. The Flemish, French-speaking, and German-speaking communities are responsible for education and cultural affairs. The Flanders, Wallonia, and Brussels regions are responsible for public works, transportation, and some social, economic, and administrative matters.

Ghent and Bruges

Bruges was the capital of medieval Flanders, and was Europe's chief wool-manufacturing town and market. It is one of the best-preserved medieval cities in Europe, and takes its name from the word for "bridge," after the bridges over its canals. Ghent remains a major center for textiles and lacemaking.

BELGIAN COUNTRYSIDE

The Belgian countryside varies greatly. The north is similar to the Netherlands: flat and laced with canals and river deltas. To the southeast are the mountains and woodlands of the Ardennes. Elsewhere there are rolling fields. Agriculture accounts for only two percent of the workforce, but occupies nearly half the country's surface area, and produces most of the country's food requirements. The temperate climate and fertile soil provide ideal conditions for growing foodstuffs, horticulture, and raising livestock. Belgium's most important rivers are the Scheldt, Sambre, and Meuse.

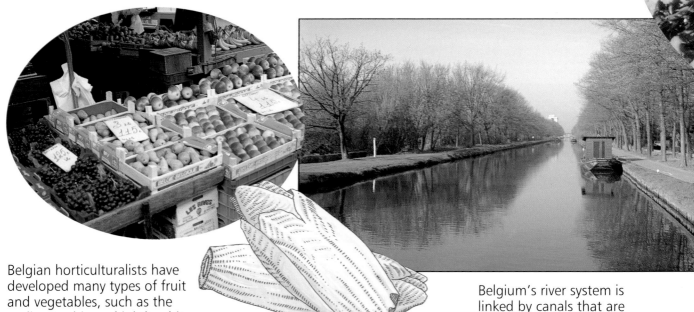

Belgian horticulturalists have developed many types of fruit and vegetables, such as the endive or chicory (right), white asparagus, Conference pears (above left), and the Brussels sprout (top of page).

Belgium's river system is linked by canals that are ideal for carrying bulky goods that do not need to travel quickly.

Coastline
Belgium's only natural frontier is its 49 miles of North Sea coastline, most of which has wide, sandy beaches. Fishermen catch shrimps by the traditional method of dragging heavy nets on horseback through the shallow water. Mussels (left) are another very popular seafood in Belgium.

What's in a face?
The painter Frans Hals (1583-1666) was born in Antwerp but spent most of his life in Haarlem in the Netherlands. He is best known for his ability to capture expressions on the faces of his subjects. Look at the painting *A Family Group* (right). How do you think the artist has conveyed the subjects' feelings toward each other?

Fish and seafood, such as crab and lobster, are popular in Belgium. Cockles and eels are considered special delicacies.

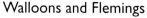

Walloons and Flemings

Belgium is divided by the 1,500-year-old "language frontier" that splits the country into French and Dutch-speaking regions, and affects all areas of Belgian life from road signs (left) to posters (below). During the 19th century, the French-speaking Walloons were dominant, as Belgian industry was concentrated in the south. As the steel industry declined, the majority Flemish population became more influential.

Spiere
Spiere - Helkijn
Espierres
Espierres - Helchin

De BBL-Kaart 12/15
JOEPIE, IK BEN ER 12!
De BBL denkt aan u...

La Carte BBL 12/15
ENFIN 12 ANS!
La BBL pense à vous...

The Ardennes

The Ardennes region in the southeast has some of Europe's most spectacular scenery. The Ardennes is Belgium's least populated area and has little agriculture, apart from some good grazing land. Its densely wooded valleys are home to a large variety of wildlife, such as wild boar, wild cats, deer (below), and pheasant. The Ardennes is particularly popular with hikers, as the mountains are not especially high but boast wonderful views. The area is also popular with skiers in the winter months. Mount Botrange, at 2,278ft, is the highest point in Belgium. Many local springs produce mineral-rich water that is bottled and exported. The town of Spa in the Ardennes has given its name to all towns with health-giving springs.

Agricultural produce

Belgian farmers grow both modern and traditional crops. One of the oldest crops is flax, which produces linseed oil, the traditional ingredient of paints. The long fibers that form the stem of the flax plant can be woven into linen, a very strong cloth. Belgium is the world's largest producer of azaleas and is Europe's largest exporter of Christmas trees. Belgian farmers also export large quantities of sugar beet and potatoes.

BELGIAN LEISURE

The Belgians have a reputation for working hard and taking life seriously. The average working week is 38-39 hours, and most people have four weeks' vacation per year. In their spare time, Belgians enjoy sports such as soccer, and during the year there are also many carnivals and processions. Education is very important in Belgium. Students spend more time at school than in almost any other country, and 25 percent of them go on to college. As Belgium is a small country surrounded by others, Belgians can easily pick up television programs from France, Germany, and Britain.

Sign for a cycle route

Education

Education is compulsory between the ages of 6 and 18, and is always in the language of the community. Belgium has two school systems: official schools, which are run by the government, and free schools, which are normally run by the Catholic Church.

Bicycles

Bicycles are the ideal form of transportation in a flat country, and cycling is very popular as a sport, too. The Belgian Eddy Merckx, nicknamed "The Cannibal," won the Tour de France a record-equalling five times.

Maigret meets Tintin

Two of the world's most published authors are Belgian, and both created famous detectives. Georges Simenon (1903-89) wrote about the pipe-smoking Jules Maigret, and Hergé (1907-83) invented Tintin, the journalist turned sleuth. Simenon published over 500 novels, while Hergé published only 24 Tintin stories, although their works have since been translated into dozens of languages and sold over 100 million copies. Hergé took his name by reversing (the sounds of) the French initials of his real name, Georges Remi.

Sports and leisure

Belgians are very keen on sports, although many prefer to watch them rather than participate. Cycling and soccer (below left) are the most popular spectator sports. On Sunday afternoons, cycle races often take place in the streets of provincial towns. One of the stranger sports is pigeon racing (above left), where pigeons are taken to a distant part of the country and have to find their way home as fast as possible. Hunting and fishing are popular, as are hiking and camping in the hills of the Ardennes.

Eating out

Many Belgians prefer their own company and that of close friends, and like to keep their home life private. Rather than invite friends to visit, they prefer to go out in the evening (see above) and enjoy a meal at a restaurant. Most Belgians are very fond of their food!

Adolphe Sax (1814-94)

Born in Dinant, Sax is best known for inventing the saxophone (right) in about 1840. He also produced other brass instruments, such as the saxhorn and the saxtuba.

Festivals and carnival

Belgium has many different festivals —the origins of some are so old that they have been forgotten. Carnival is held just before Lent, a last celebration before 40 days of abstinence. At Mons, there is a re-enactment of St. George's battle with the dragon. For 500 years, the clowns of Binche (right) have paraded with ostrich feathers to mark the arrival of the first South American Indians in Europe. At Ypres, in the Festival of the Cats, model cats and witches are thrown into the crowd. There are also Belgian festivals to celebrate the harvest.

Cooking beef carbonnade

A carbonnade used to mean a dish that was grilled or boiled over the coals, but now means a stew. It is a typically Flemish meal. Try this recipe for yourself:

First, cut 675g of chuck steak into squares and brown it in 125g of butter. Then remove the meat and soften 450g of chopped onions in the butter. Place the meat and onions in a heavy pan. Add 330ml of beer and some beef stock. Stir some flour into the fat remaining in the pan, together with a little more stock (you need about 330ml of stock in total), and stir until it thickens.

Finally, add the mixture to the meat, season with a tablespoon of brown sugar, salt, and pepper. Cover and cook gently for two hours, et voilà!, a delicious meal for four.

BELGIAN RESOURCES

Belgium was swift to industrialize, yet today its prosperity is based on services, which employ over 70 percent of the workforce. Its location has made it a major trading nation, and it is heavily dependent on international trade as it has few natural resources of its own. Almost two-thirds of all economic activity takes place in Flanders. The most important industries are metallurgy, machine and motor construction, food, and chemicals.

Import—export
International trade is so important to the Belgian economy that one Belgian in two works for the export industry, and more than 50 percent of national production is exported. Belgium imports raw materials, like iron ore, and exports finished or semi-finished products, such as steel and machinery. Belgium's steel industry used to be based near the coalfields in Wallonia. These mines are now exhausted, and today the industry is oil-powered, so the steel plants have been moved to Flanders near the oil ports. This move shifted the power balance between Walloons and Flemings.

Although in the past the Belgian economy relied heavily on its steel industry, today's diverse economy is a combination of high quality technology and traditional craftsmanship, producing everything from lasers and modern synthetic fibers, to lace and crystal glass.

Diamond cutting
A Belgian master cutter may examine an uncut diamond for weeks before cutting it. The rough diamond is held in a "dop" or shell. An incision is made, and the diamond is then expertly split (below left). To create each facet, the tiny surfaces that make diamonds sparkle, the stone is held against a diamond dusted disk at a precise angle (below right).

Antwerp port
Antwerp (above right) on the Scheldt River, is 55 miles from the sea, but it is still Europe's second largest port. It became a major port in the 15th century, when the larger port at Bruges became blocked by storms. By the early 16th century, Antwerp was full of foreign businesses dealing with the rest of Europe. Water transport is still vital to Belgium's economy, with more than 1,240 miles of inland waterways. Antwerp handles over 20,000 ships each year, from over 800 other ports, and claims to be the fastest in the world at unloading and reloading ships.

A photographic pioneer

Lieven Gevaert (1868-1935) was a pioneer in the field of photography, especially in producing photographic materials. Born in Antwerp, he combined his skills as an inventor and businessman to improve the quality of photography and make it accessible to more people.

Euros (right)

The appealing design and bright colors of these old Gevaert film boxes made them easily identifiable.

Belgian scientists

Abbé Lemaître (1894-1966), an astrophysicist and priest, developed the Big Bang theory to explain the origin of the universe. He believed that all matter was once condensed in an unimaginably dense state, and has been expanding ever since. Etienne Lenoir (1822-1900) invented the first practical internal combustion gas engine (below). Leo Baekeland (1863-1944) emigrated to the U.S., where he invented Bakelite, a forerunner of modern plastics.

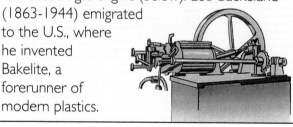

Holy beers

The Belgians have long been great brewers, and today produce hundreds of different brands of beer. The recipes are often several hundred years old, and are well-kept secrets. In the Middle Ages, breweries were often run by monks. The abbeys encouraged the science of brewing, and introduced hops to flavor the beer.

Lacemaking

Belgian lace, made from linen or cotton, has been prized for centuries. Made by twisting and braiding bobbins, it originated in Flanders in the 16th century and requires great craftsmanship and patience to make. By 1600, it was a luxury product worn by men and women. With the invention of a machine that copied handmade lace around 1840, prices fell, and demand increased dramatically. From 1850 to 1914, an estimated 20,000 lacemakers were based in the towns of Bruges, Ghent, and Brussels. Today, handmade lace is largely sold as a souvenir item.

DUTCH CITIES

The Netherlands is one of world's most densely populated countries. Most of the population is concentrated in the Randstad, a conurbation in the west of the country, where most of the industry is also located. Each of the four major cities, all within the Randstad, have a population of over 200,000. Though the population is growing, a strong Dutch reaction to tower blocks has led to a synthesis of old and new architecture (see the traditional bridge, above left, and modern housing, below left). The Dutch capital is Amsterdam, but its seat of government is in The Hague.

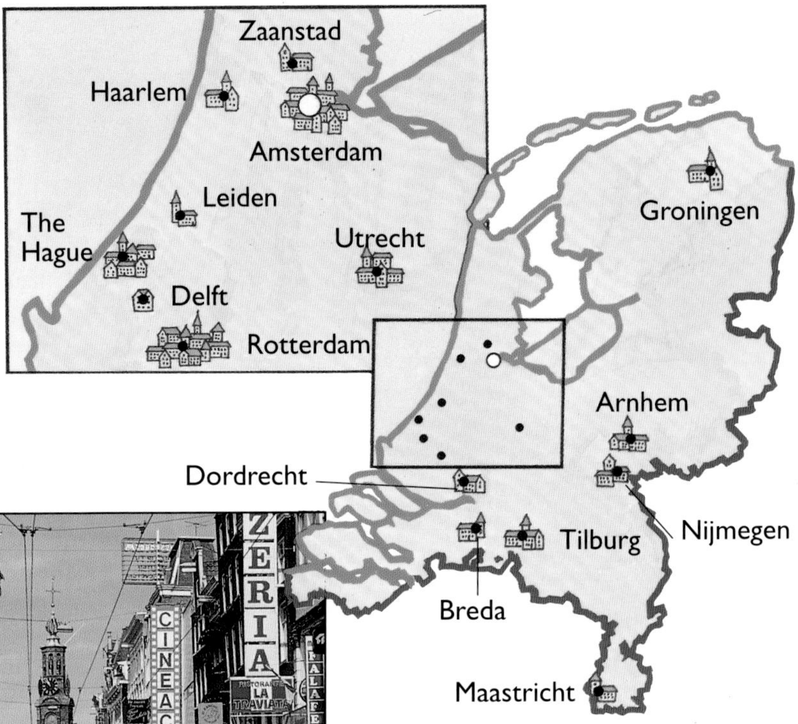

Amsterdam
Many of Amsterdam's streets are waterways lined with 17th-century houses, earning it the nickname "the Venice of the North." It is an important cultural center with many famous museums, a rich nightlife, characterful bars, and a notorious red-light area.

A bustling street in Amsterdam reveals the contrast of old buildings and modern city life.

Double Dutch?
A few Dutch words have made the leap into the English language such as brandy, skate, skipper, and yacht. The word "yankee," used to describe people from the northern states of the U.S., may have begun as a nickname for Dutch colonists who arrived there. Cookie comes from the Dutch *koekje*.

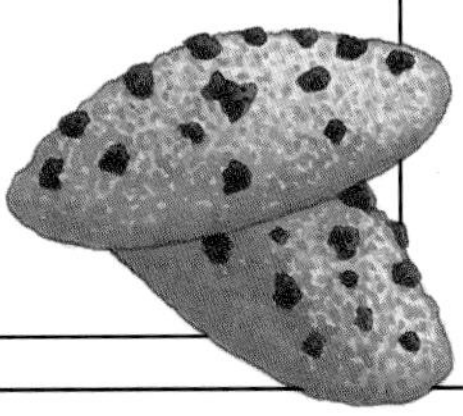

Religious differences
For centuries, religion played a key part in the division of Dutch society. Since the Second World War, these divisions (known as *verzuiling*) have faded, but even today, being a Protestant or Catholic can influence one's choice of newspaper, political party, school, or hospital. While Catholics represent just over 30 percent of the population, and Protestants just over 20 percent, an even larger percentage of the Dutch now claim no religious affiliation.

Map labels: Zaanstad, Haarlem, Amsterdam, Leiden, The Hague, Utrecht, Delft, Rotterdam, Groningen, Arnhem, Nijmegen, Tilburg, Breda, Dordrecht, Maastricht

Traditional architecture

Amsterdam's elegant *gracht* houses (right) are deliberately narrow. Rich merchants demanded that their houses had access to the gracht (which provided drinking water), so the gable-fronted houses were tightly packed to make the most of the limited space. Even so, there is plenty of room inside, as the houses run a long way back. Amsterdam lies on marshy ground, so deep piles have to be driven to provide solid foundations.

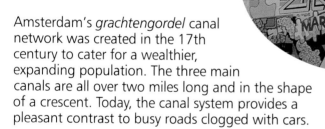

Street art

Dutch cities house many famous art museums, and the country has a long artistic tradition, although street art has few links in common with the past. While many consider such urban decorations colorful and inspired, others prefer their art to be more conventional. In busy cities, cycles are often painted in individual ways in an attempt to deter bicycle thieves.

Amsterdam's *grachtengordel* canal network was created in the 17th century to cater for a wealthier, expanding population. The three main canals are all over two miles long and in the shape of a crescent. Today, the canal system provides a pleasant contrast to busy roads clogged with cars.

Mata Hari, secret agent

Mata Hari was the stage name of Margarethe Geertruida Zelle (1876-1917), a Dutch dancer. During the First World War, she seduced many high-ranking officials and leaked Allied secrets to the Germans. She may have been a double agent for both France and Germany, but was eventually shot by the French for espionage.

DUTCH COUNTRYSIDE

Fewer than four percent of the Dutch population work in agriculture and fishing, although half the land in the Netherlands is cultivated and provides large surpluses for the export of crops. Agriculture ranges from bulb growing (above) and dairy farms, to the fruit farms of the Gelderland province. Half of the Netherlands is below sea level, and much of the land is reclaimed from the sea. The provinces are made up partly of intensively farmed countryside, where people live in modest gabled houses, and partly in garden suburbs, where new towns lie in the midst of rape fields and the inhabitants commute to the big cities.

Profits in the fishing industry (below) have fallen over recent years as overfishing has reduced stocks. Dutch fishermen trawl for herring, mackerel, and cod in the North Sea. In the Irish Sea, they fish for flat fish, such as plaice and sole, with boats called cutters, and in Danish and German waters they fish for shrimp. Shellfish are caught in the Eastern Scheldt and the Waddenzee.

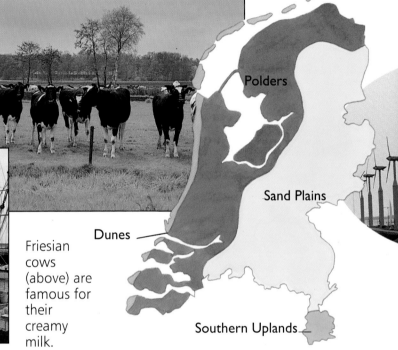

Polders

Sand Plains

Dunes

Southern Uplands

Friesian cows (above) are famous for their creamy milk.

Strange pastimes
A number of unusual pastimes are found in the Netherlands, and especially in Friesland. One of these is the *Elfstedentocht*, a 78-mile skating race over the frozen canals linking 11 towns. As many as 18,000 competitors take part. Pole vaulting over dikes is called *fierljeppen*, and competitors who don't make it get a drenching. *Wadlopen*, or walking over mudflats at low tide, is also popular in the summer months.

Land reclamation
The Dutch have reclaimed so much land from the sea that, according to an old saying, "God created the world, but the Dutch created Holland." Dutch history is tied to the struggle against the sea, and since the Middle Ages they have been reclaiming land by building dikes, or raised earth banks, around a lake. Water used to be pumped from the lake into a canal by windmills—this is now done by diesel pumps. The land that is left is called a polder (right), and is often very fertile. In the 1930s, the 18-mile Barrier Dam was built across the Zuider Zee, creating the new province of Flevoland and the IJsselmeer Lake.

Windmills

To make a model windmill, take two pieces of thin cardboard (1.5in x 3in). Fold them lengthwise, so that one side overlaps the other. Push the overlapping edges together and tape them together, so one side is curved. Glue them to a straw, with the curved face up (see diagram), and tape another straw at right angles, to use as a spindle. Push this through a hole in an old drinks carton (see diagram).

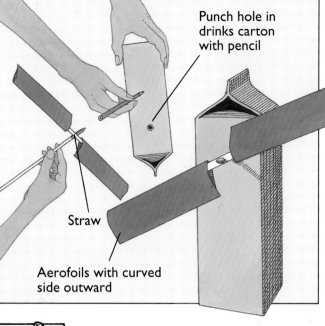

Punch hole in drinks carton with pencil

Straw

Aerofoils with curved side outward

Old and new: traditional windmills and modern wind farms (left)

Different regions

The Netherlands has four main land regions: the Dunes, which curve around the North Sea coast; the Polders; the Sand Plains, a rolling agricultural and forested area; and the Southern Uplands, around Maastricht.

Cheese

The Dutch cheese Gouda is sold in four forms, as bacteria in the cheese causes it to change with age. *Jong* is a creamy cheese, *belegen* is four months old, *oud* is 10 months old, while *overbelegen* is a crumbly old cheese. Edam, with its famous red paraffin coat, was originally brushed with vermilion to distinguish it from other cheeses.

Dike   Reclaimed land   Dike   Sea

Regional dress and clogs

Many of the simple and practical Dutch traditional costumes are still worn in rural areas. Zeeland, once inhabited by farmers and merchants, has the most sumptuous costumes, as the skippers brought back expensive materials from abroad. A million *klompen*, or clogs, are sold every year to Friesians, who wear them as everyday shoes. These clogs are light and strong, unlike those in souvenir shops (right).

DUTCH LEISURE

Approximately one-third of the Dutch population are members of sports clubs. Soccer, hockey, tennis, and sailing are all popular, and many people skate on the frozen canals during the winter. Since the 17th century, Dutch artists from Rembrandt (left) to Van Gogh have exhibited a distinctive national character in their paintings. Education is very important in the Netherlands, and the roots of the education system can be traced back to the Batavian Republic, the state established in the Low Countries by Napoléon.

Education

Students begin secondary school at 11. There are many different types of secondary school, which help train students for jobs, or prepare them for college. Leiden University, which was founded in 1575, is the oldest and most renowned in the Netherlands.

Education is compulsory in the Netherlands between the ages of 5 and 16, although it is possible to start school at 4.

Food

Dutch food is traditionally simple and wholesome, with different breads, plenty of vegetables, meat, and fish, and lots of dairy produce. Warming dishes like *hutspot* (carrots, onions, and potatoes mashed together) are especially good for bitter winters. Herrings are another speciality, traditionally eaten by holding the tail and dropping them into the mouth (left).

Environmental concerns

The Dutch are a very environmentally-conscious nation, and the headquarters of Greenpeace, the international campaigning organization, is in Amsterdam. One campaign, launched in 1990 under the slogan "A better environment starts with you," spread the message that everybody could help. It encouraged people to buy environmentally friendly products, to separate kitchen and garden waste from household garbage, and use a bicycle instead of the car. There are now over 11 million bicycles (above) in the Netherlands. Some people even move house by means of an old-fashioned *bakfiets* or baker's bicycle!

Royal family

Crowned in 1980, Queen Beatrix is the head of state of the Netherlands, Aruba, and the Antilles. The monarchy is extremely popular, partly because the House of Orange was closely linked to the struggle for independence, and partly because the modern royal family are regarded as being very down-to-earth—the Dutch people tend to mock any *camponses* (self-importance).

Sports

Soccer is the most popular sport in the Netherlands. The Dutch international side is renowned for attacking, imaginative soccer, and has produced many great players, such as Johan Cruyff, "the Flying Dutchman," Ruud Gullit (below), famous for his dreadlocked headers, and Ruud van Nistelrooy. Athletics, swimming, riding bicycles, and tennis are all popular, as are water sports like sailing (above). Walking events, such as the Nijmegen marathon, are highly organized, but are as much communal activities as competitive sports. In some towns in Zeeland, *krulbollen*, a form of bowling, is played, while in Friesland there are *skutjeslien*, races in flat-bottomed sailing boats.

The Dutch masters

The Netherlands has produced an astonishing number of world-class artists for such a small nation. The works of Dutch 16th- and 17th-century masters, such as Hieronymous Bosch, Rembrandt, Hals, and Vermeer (his painting *The Lacemaker* is shown below left), command fortunes on the international art market. In the 19th and 20th centuries, artists like Van Gogh (1853-90) and Mondrian broke new ground artistically, although it wasn't always recognized during their lifetimes. Vincent Van Gogh's *Sunflowers* is among the world's most famous pictures, but Vincent sold only one painting during his lifetime—to his brother—and killed himself at the scene of his last work. Below right is Van Gogh's painting *The Lilac Bush*.

DUTCH RESOURCES

The Netherlands has exploited its location in Europe to become a major trading nation. Standing at the mouths of the Rhine, Maas, and Waal Rivers, the country plays a leading part in world trade, and Rotterdam is the world's busiest port. Major industries are food, alcohol, tobacco, chemicals, oil refining, and metallurgy. The Netherlands is also Europe's largest supplier of natural gas. Today, famous firms such as Akzo, Unilever, Shell, and Philips (a respected electronics innovator) fly the Dutch flag abroad.

Energy

The Netherlands is Europe's largest producer and supplier of natural gas, most of which comes from the North Sea. Approximately 95 percent of homes are connected to the gas network, and it is also used to generate electricity. The Netherlands produces some of its own oil, but the refineries at Rotterdam use oil brought from around the world. The government promotes a variety of energy-saving campaigns and also invests in the search for alternative energy sources, such as wind power (see wind farms on p. 21).

Two young Dutch aviators set up firms in 1919—Albert Plesman, who founded KLM, the Royal Dutch Airlines (above), and Anthony Fokker, whose company went on to provide instruments for both the Giotto space probe and the Ariane rocket program. Two Anglo-Dutch industrial giants are Shell (left), a petroleum and agrochemicals company, and Unilever, producers of soaps and detergents.

Euros

Waterways

The Netherlands' 2,690 miles of navigable canals and waterways carry goods deep into the European mainland, or ship them out for export around the world. Rotterdam (center of spread) is accessible to the world's largest tankers, and is also the port with the largest turnover (over 300 million tons of goods a year) in the world. Of all the goods loaded or unloaded in the European Union (EU), 30 percent pass through Dutch ports. Dutch carriers perform about half of all water trade in the EU, and the Netherlands has more rivercraft than any other country. Canals also help drain the country's low-lying land, and boost tourism as they are an attractive part of the landscape.

Dutch canals are a great way for tourists to get around.

Delftware

Delft, in the western Netherlands, is famous for its distinctive porcelain (a mixture of clays that becomes translucent when fired). Although the town had produced pottery for many years, when traders brought porcelain back from China in the early 1600s, potters started to copy the blue and white designs. By the mid-17th century, there were Delft vases and bowls everywhere, decorated with landscapes, flowers, ships, and portraits.

Philips

The Philips company of Eindhoven is one of the most familiar names in the field of audio and visual technology. When it started in 1892 the firm produced carbon-filament lamps, but since the Second World War its research department (left) has made numerous technological

breakthroughs such as the compact cassette, the video recorder, the compact disk and, more recently, the interactive CD-i system. Today, it is also a major producer of optical communications systems, medical technology, personal electronics, and domestic appliances.

Tulip flowers are only left to stand for ten days to maintain nutrients in the soil.

Tulips

The Netherlands, known as the florist of Europe, exports more flowers than the rest of the world combined. The tulip, which probably came from China originally, now attracts thousands of tourists to the famous tulip fields between Leiden and Haarlem (left). Modern techniques, such as growing cuttings in test tubes, are increasingly common. With this method, up to one million disease-free seedlings a year can be grown from a single healthy plant.

LUXEMBOURG

Luxembourg is an independent sovereign state. In the north of the country are the beautiful Ardennes hills, and to the east is the grape-growing Moselle valley. The south is mainly rolling farmland although the old mining region is also here. About a third of the country is forested. Thanks to the wealth created by industry and finance, Luxembourg has one of the highest standards of living in Europe. Its name comes from Anglo-Saxon, and means "little fortress."

Country

The northern part of Luxembourg, known as the Osling, consists of forested hills, meandering rivers, and narrow valleys. The Gutland in the south (right) is a more gentle landscape of woodland, lush meadows, and vineyards. Ruined castles and charming villages dot the countryside.

Luxembourg city

Luxembourg's capital

Luxembourg city was founded by the Romans, as its dramatic situation over the gorges of the Alzette and Pétrusse Rivers made it easy to defend. The fortress was destroyed in 1554 by a gunpowder explosion. Today, Luxembourg is a peaceful city of café-lined streets and picturesque parks.

Three languages

As a tiny country, Luxembourg has long understood the need to communicate with its neighbors. As a result, the people of Luxembourg commonly speak at least three languages. Letzeburgesch is the most common everyday language, French is used in most elementary schools, and German in most secondary schools. Newspapers are in German, and French is used in parliament. Many people speak English fluently, too.

Grand Duchy

Luxembourg was established as an independent state in 963. The Duchy of Luxembourg was established in 1354. The title of grand duke is hereditary, its holders belonging to the House of Nassau. Like Belgium, Luxembourg spent many centuries under the control of France, Spain, and Austria. In 1815, it became part of the Netherlands, then in 1830 declared its independence. During both world wars, it was occupied by the Germans.

26

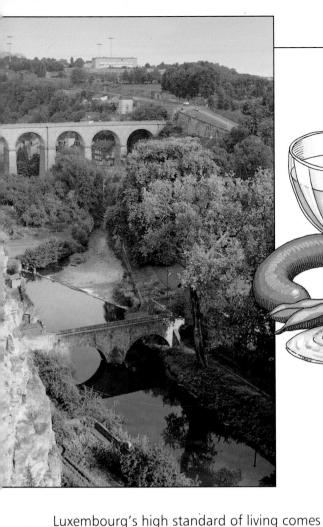

Euros

Food and drink

Farmers in the Bon Pays, or Gutland, region grow barley, oats, potatoes, and wheat. On the pastureland, there are large herds of cattle and sheep. Pork is a favorite food, in dishes such as Treipen (black pudding), smoked pork with broad beans, and Ardennes ham. Kachkeis is one of several local cheeses and is often eaten with fruit or grain liqueurs. Beer and white wine from the Moselle valley are popular, too.

Luxembourg's high standard of living comes from its financial sector and thriving iron and steel industry. Because of its favorable laws governing banking secrecy and taxation, it is home to more than 260 banks, including the European Investment Bank. It has a very comprehensive welfare system that redistributes over half of government income, and unemployment and inflation are low. Education is compulsory from the ages of 6 to 15, and at 12 children go either to secondary schools or technical colleges.

Redouté (1759-1840)

Born in St. Hubert in the Ardennes, Pierre-Joseph Redouté began at the age of 13 a career that was to make him the most influential botanical artist of all time. In Paris, he worked for Josephine Bonaparte, creating over 600 vellum drawings that are still studied today.

An independent spirit

The people of Luxembourg are independent and content, as expressed in the line from their national anthem *Ons Hemecht* (Our Homeland) which runs *Mir welle bleiwe wat mir sin*, and means "We want to remain what we are." Luxembourg is sometimes seen as a model for a future Europe— a truly cosmopolitan place that has maintained its individuality.

TODAY AND TOMORROW

Home to many important world and European organizations, the Benelux countries are well placed to take advantage of European union. As small countries with a history of foreign interference, they are used to dealing with their neighbors and adapting quickly to changing needs. Although language differences will continue to create tension, the fiercely independent cultures and healthy economies of all three countries will ensure that their influence continues to be felt across the globe.

Center of power

The Benelux countries manage to exert such a strong influence worldwide partly because they are home to so many important international organizations. The World Trade Center is in Rotterdam (top of page), NATO (North Atlantic Treaty Organization), and the European Parliament are in Brussels, and the European Court of Justice and other European Union buildings (above right) are situated in Luxembourg city.

The European Union

Under the Treaty of Maastricht, EU member countries have agreed to new levels of cooperation on money and social matters.

Flag of the European Union

United Nations

The Benelux countries are founder members of the United Nations, set up to maintain peace and security and to solve members' social and economic problems.

Maastricht

The Benelux countries are fervent pro-Europeans, and well understand the advantages of working together with their neighbors. The Maastricht Treaty, signed in 1992 in the Dutch city of that name, committed the member nations of the European Union to work toward greater unity in the future, and gave increased powers to the European Parliament (right) in Brussels.

The European Parliament

The liberal tradition

The Netherlands has a long tradition of liberalism and tolerance, stretching back to the 16th century. Also influenced by the youthful counterculture of the 60s, the Dutch believe that a relaxed, open attitude toward drugs reduces abuse—there are even "smoking" cafés for soft-drug users. This is all part of a general live-and-let-live attitude. The Dutch have also had more success than other nations in controlling hard drugs.

Tourism

Tourism is an important sector of the economy in the Benelux countries. The canals and islands of the Netherlands, the medieval cities of Belgium, and the spectacular forests and river valleys of Luxembourg provide a variety unmatched in such a small area anywhere else in Europe. All these attractions are easily reached by excellent highways, railroads, and rivers.

The Enkhuizen Zuider Zee Museum in the Netherlands

NATO

The Benelux countries signed the North Atlantic Treaty in 1949, which stated that an attack against any member would be considered an attack against all members.

ESA

Belgium and the Netherlands are both members of the European Space Agency, established to develop a space program in Europe.

The struggle against the sea

The Dutch and the Belgians of Flanders have centuries of experience in the fight against the sea. Although their expertise has produced some of the most ingenious engineering solutions for holding back the sea and turning the water into land, they now face another problem. Global warming is threatening to increase the temperature of the world, and to melt some of the ice at the polar caps. If the sea level rises by only several feet, then the area below sea level in the Netherlands, which is home to 60 percent of the population, may be under threat.

In spite of centuries of foreign rule, Belgium, the Netherlands, and Luxembourg have each carved a unique identity for themselves. Since the Second World War, their economic union has allowed them to establish economic stability and a good standard of living— a solid platform for future prosperity.

FACTS AND FIGURES

THE NETHERLANDS

Name: Koninkrijk der Nederlanden (Kingdom of the Netherlands)

Capital: Amsterdam

National anthem: *Wilhelmus van Nassouwe* ("William of Nassau")

Official language: Dutch; in the province of Friesland, Friesian is also used as an official language.

Currency: The euro replaced the guilder in 2002.

Population: 16.1 million

Population density: 745 persons per sq mile

Distribution: 89% urban, 11% rural

BELGIUM

Name: Royaume de Belgique (in French) or Koninkrijk België (in Flemish)

Capital: Brussels

National anthem: *La Brabançonne* ("The Brabant Song")

Official languages: Flemish (form of Dutch), French, and German.

Currency: As of 2002, the euro, previously the Belgian franc

Population: 10.2 million

Population density: 538 persons per sq mile

LUXEMBOURG

Name: Grand-Duché de Luxembourg

Capital: Luxembourg city

National anthem: Ons Hemecht ("Our Homeland")

Official languages: French, German, and Letzeburgesch. Letzeburgesch, a dialect of German with many French words, was recognized as an official language in 1984.

Currency: As of 2002, the euro, previously the Luxembourg franc

Population: 454,000

Population density: 264 per sq mile

Cheese from Edam

Flowers from province of south Holland

Pottery from Delft

The Netherlands

Groningen oil fields

Salt from Hengel

Dairy produce and livestock from Dutch sand plains

Lace from Ghent

Flax and textile industry, and hop-growing in Flanders

Wallonia, former home of coal and steel industries

Belgium

Flanders, new home of steel industry

Coal from southern uplands

Timber from Ardennes

Steel from Luxembourg

Lux.

Ethnic groups: Dutch 83%, other 17% (of which 9% are from Turkey and Morocco and former colonies in Indonesia, Surinam, and the Netherlands Antilles.

Religion: Roman Catholic 31%, Protestant 21%, no religious affiliation 40%, Muslim 4.4 %, other 3.6%

Area: 13,104 sq miles

Size: north–south 196 miles, east–west 162 miles

Highest point: Mount Vaalserberg, 1053ft above sea level

Lowest point: Prins Alexander Polder, 22ft below sea level

Ethnic groups: Fleming 58%, Walloon 31%, mixed or other 11%

Religion: Roman Catholic 88%, Muslim 2.5%, Protestant 1%, other 8.5%

Area: 11,787 sq miles

Size: east–west 170 miles, north–south 140 miles

Highest point: Botrange Mountain, 2,277ft above sea level

Lowest point: Sea level

Ethnic groups: Luxembourger 66%, Portuguese 12%, Italian 5%, French 4%, Belgian 3%, German 2%, other 8%

Religion: Roman Catholic 87%, some Protestants, Jews, and Muslims.

Area: 998 sq miles

Size: north–south 55 miles, east–west 35 miles

Highest point: Burgplatz, 1,834ft above sea level

Lowest point: Moselle River, 436ft above sea level

THE NETHERLANDS

Coastlines: North Sea to the north-west (228 miles)

Main rivers: Rhine, Maas, Waal, and Scheldt

Climate: As Belgium

Location/physical features: Four main regions—The Dunes, 14 to 24ft above sea level, along the entire North Sea coast, mainly sand; The Polders, mostly below sea level and protected by dikes, but most productive farmlands and biggest cities; The Sand Plains in the southeast, less than 98ft above sea level, landscape of pine forests and clay soils (near rivers); and Southern Uplands, the highest land region with fertile soils where much fruit is grown in orchards.

Crop production: (tons) Potatoes 7.3 million, sugar beets 7.6 million, wheat 1.2 million, apples 570,000, tomatoes 525,000, cucumbers 500,000, onions 453,000, barley 218,000.

Livestock: Pigs 14 million, cattle 4.5 million, sheep 1.7 million.

Main industries: Agroindustries, metal and engineering products (below right); electrical machinery and equipment; chemicals; petroleum; construction; microelectronics.

Main imports: Machinery and transportation equipment; food and live animals; foodstuffs; clothing; chemicals; minerals and fuels.

Main exports: Machinery and transportation equipment; chemicals; food and live animals; minerals and fuels.

BELGIUM

Coastlines: North Sea to the north-west (39 miles)

Main rivers: Scheldt, Sambre, Meuse

Climate: Moderate marine climate, marked by mild winters with little frost, fairly cool summers, and a good deal of wind and rain.

Location/physical features: There are four main land regions—the coastal and interior lowlands in the north protected from the sea by dikes; the Kempenland in the northeast (traditionally covered in birch forests), the central low plateaus with the country's best agricultural land and large cities, such as Brussels; and the Ardennes, an area of forest-covered hills separated by winding rivers.

Crop production: (tons) Sugar beets 5.2 million, potatoes 2.5 million, wheat 1.9 million, barley 435,500. Other important crops include fruits, tomatoes, and flax.

Livestock: Pigs 7 million, cattle 3 million, sheep 161,000, horses 24,000.

Main industries: Engineering and metal products; processed food and beverages; chemicals; basic metals; textiles; glass; plastics; petroleum; coal.

Main imports: Machinery and transportation equipment; chemicals and related products; metals; foodstuffs and live animals; diamonds; minerals, and fuels.

Main exports: Machinery and transportation equipment; chemicals; diamonds; metals; foodstuffs.

LUXEMBOURG

Coastlines: Luxembourg has no coastline.

Main rivers: Moselle, Sure, Alzette

Climate: As Belgium

Location/physical features: Luxembourg is divided into two regions: Osling in the north of the country is a wooded, hilly region of great natural beauty; Gutland in the south is pastureland.

Crop production: (tons) Barley 63,300, wheat 52,800, potatoes 22,800, rye 16,800, oats 11,800, sugar beets 10,400, apples 5,600.

Livestock: Cattle 214,000, pigs 76,600.

Main industries: Banking; iron and steel; food processing; chemicals; metal products; engineering; tires; glass; aluminum.

Main imports: Minerals; metals; foodstuffs; quality consumer goods.

Major import sources: Belgium 29.7%, Germany 23%, France 13.2%, Taiwan 6.7%, The Netherlands 4.6%.

Main exports: Machinery and equipment; steel products; chemicals; rubber products; plastics; textiles; gas.

Major export destinations: Germany 23.9%, France 20%, Belgium 10.5%, UK 8.7%, Italy 6.1%, Spain 4.5%, The Netherlands 4.4%..

ECONOMY

The GDP (gross domestic product) is the amount of goods and services produced within a country. By dividing the GDP by the population a *per capita* result is reached.

Figures shown are the GDP per capita in the year 2002 (GDPs are shown in U.S. dollars).

Luxembourg	44,586
Belgium	28,964
Netherlands	27,011
U.S.	35,935
Germany	26,234
U.K.	25,427
Italy	24,915
Spain	20,660

FAMOUS FACES

WRITERS

SCIENTISTS

Desiderius Erasmus (1466-1536, right), born in Rotterdam, was one of the most influential figures in the Renaissance. His hostility to the Catholic Church helped pave the way for the Reformation.

Georges Simenon (1903-89). See page 14.

Benedictus de Spinoza (1632-77), born in Amsterdam, was a Dutch-Jewish philosopher, and one of the greatest thinkers of the 17th century.

Anne Frank (1929-45, left). See page 9.

Count Maurice Maeterlinck (1862-1949), born in Ghent, was a Belgian dramatist. He wrote many philosophical works, and won the Nobel Prize for literature in 1911.

Hergé (Georges Remi, 1907-83). See page 14.

Anton van Leeuwenhoek (1632-1723, right). Born at Delft, he became a famous microscopist, and made important discoveries concerning the circulation of the blood, blood corpuscles, and the skin.

Leo Baekeland (1863-1944). See page 17.

Abbé Lemaître (1894-1966). See page 17.

Hugo de Vries (1848-1935) was a Dutch botanist, born at Haarlem, who developed theories of plant genetics and evolutionary theory.

Andreas Vesalius (1514-64, left) was a Belgian anatomist, born in Brussels. He advanced studies of biology and anatomy with his descriptions of bones and the nervous system, discovered by dissecting cadavers. The Inquisition sentenced him to death for "body snatching," later commuted to a pilgrimage to Jerusalem.

Christiaan Huygens (1629-93, right), born in The Hague, was an important physicist. Among his many achievements and discoveries, he developed the pendulum clock, following Galileo's theory, and discovered the rings of Saturn.

Marie Eugene Dubois (1858-1940). Born at Eijsden, Holland, he discovered "Java man," which he claimed was the missing link between apes and man. After initial ridicule, his views became accepted, although by then, Dubois was convinced the bones were of a giant gibbon.

MUSICIANS

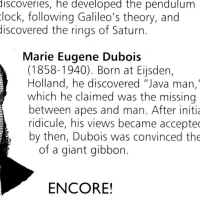

Roland de Lassus (1532-94) was a Flemish composer. He trained in Italy, and joined the court of Duke Albrecht of Bavaria. His madrigals and chansons made him famous throughout Europe.

Cesar Auguste Franck (1822-90, right), a composer, was born in Liège into a German family. He began as a pianist, and his compositions were originally considered too daring, until a number of established musicians, including Liszt, championed him. His reputation is based on a few pieces written after the age of 50.

Adolphe Sax (1814-94, below left). See page 15.

ENCORE!

Gerardus Mercator (1512-94, below left), was a Flemish geographer and mapmaker. The Mercator projection is still used for nautical charts. He published the first part of a world "Atlas," the first time the term had been used. The book was so-called because it had Atlas holding a globe on the cover.

Jacques Brel (1929-78). Singer and songwriter, born in Brussels but settled in Paris. Known for his lyrical sharpness and passionate voice, his songs include *Ne Me Quitte Pas*, *Mathilde*, and *Amsterdam*.

Audrey Hepburn (1929-93, right). Born in Brussels to Dutch and British parents, Audrey Hepburn's real name was Edda Hepburn van Heemstra. She trained as a ballet dancer but found fame as an actress, winning an Oscar for her role in *Roman Holiday* (1953).

PAINTERS

Belgium and the Netherlands have produced many fine artists. Jan van Eyck (1385-1441) was the first to use native landscapes as backdrops for biblical scenes. Hieronymous Bosch (1460-1516) painted gruesome visions of hell and hideous beasts. Peter Paul Rubens (1577-1640, below right), traveled to Italy to study the Renaissance artists, and became the most influential artist of the 17th century. His dynamic pictures and energetic figures caused a sensation. As the Netherlands grew rich in the 17th century, merchants commissioned many paintings. The Renaissance brought changes in painting techniques, and the way the human body was painted became more important than the subject.

(Above) *The Garden of Earthly Delights* by Hieronymous Bosch.

After the Reformation in the Netherlands, the Calvinists forbade religious paintings. Artists therefore painted different subjects, such as scenes from everyday life, landscapes, and still lifes.

(Below) *Man in Armor* by Rembrandt van Rijn.

One of the most original artists was Rembrandt van Rijn (1606-69, above left). As a young man, he was extremely popular, but his later pictures upset his patrons and he died bitter and bankrupt.

Vermeer (1632-75) was known for the peace and intimacy of his pictures, and the trademark of Frans Hals (1585-1666) was his ability to capture a facial expression.

As the prosperity of the Netherlands waned in the 18th century, so did the quality and originality of its art. The 19th century produced Vincent Van Gogh (left), although he didn't receive recognition until after his death. Popular 20th-century artists were Piet Mondrian (1872-1944), with his celebrated grids, and Belgian René Magritte (1898-1967), who depicted surreal, dreamlike scenes of strange objects in unlikely places.

INDEX

Photocredits
Abbreviations: l-left, r-right, b-bottom, t-top, c-center, m-middle
Front cover both, back cover — Digital Stock. 1, 2m, 2b, 3, 4t, 4b, 5m, 5b, 8-9, 10 all, 11m, 11bl, 12 all, 13t, 13tl, 14c, 18 all, 19tr, 19m, 20 all, 21, 22 all, 22-23, 23t, 24tr, 24b, 25tr, 25b — Select Pictures. 2t, 4b, 5t, 9m, 13tr, 14tl, 14ml, 14mr, 14b, 15, 16m, 19b, 24tl, 24-25, 29m, 31 — Frank Spooner Pictures. 6-7, 11tr, 12-13b, 23b, 27br, 33 both — Bridgeman Art Library. 7 both, 8m — Mary Evans Picture Library. 8b — US Airforce. 11br, 27bl — Eye Ubiquitous. 16tl, 16-17, 26 both, 26-27, 27bm, 28tl, 28m — Spectrum Colour Library. 17t, 28br — Roger Vlitos. 17tr, 24mr, 27tr — PBD. 17b — Paul Nightingale.

25m — Philips. 28bl — Universal Pictorial Press & Agency Ltd.